Zion

OF

30 Devotions on the Family of Jesus

Judah

ISBN 978-1-0877-5207-5
Item 005834384
Dewey Decimal Classification Number: 242
Subject Heading: DEVOTIONAL LITERATURE / BIBLE STUDY AND TEACHING / GOD

Printed in the United States of America

Student Ministry Publishing
Lifeway Resources
One Lifeway Plaza
Nashville, Tennessee 37234

We believe that the Bible has God for its author; salvation for its end; and truth, without any mixture of error, for its matter and that all Scripture is totally true and trustworthy. To review Lifeway's doctrinal guideline, please visit www.lifeway.com/doctrinalguideline.

Unless otherwise noted, all Scripture quotations are taken from the Christian Standard Bible®, Copyright © 2017 by Holman Bible Publishers. Used by permission. Christian Standard Bible® and CSB® are federally registered trademarks of Holman Bible Publishers.

PUBLISHING TEAM

Director, Student Ministry
Ben Trueblood

Manager, Student Ministry Publishing
John Paul Basham

Editorial Team Leader
Karen Daniel

Writer
Leslie Hudson

Content Editor
Kyle Wiltshire

Production Editor
Brooke Hill

Graphic Designer
Shiloh Stufflebeam

TABLE OF CONTENTS

INTRO

Every family is different, and even people raised in the same family look at their relatives and experiences through different lenses over time. Some families are close; some can't get far enough away from each other. Some families thrive on chaos, noise, and laughter; some enjoy simplicity and quiet. Some families gather many generations under one roof as often as possible; some don't even know those outside their own homes.

No matter the type, our families shape us. The genes we received—not only from our parents but from their parents and the generations of parents before them—play a tiny role in what we look like, how crooked our teeth are, our eye and hair color, and how tall we are. Family lines usually run through blood, but every now and then, a family is changed through marriage, adoption, and the blending of families.

On top of that, your home shapes you. Where you grew up—city or country, north or south, hot or cold—all of it helped shape you. In the question of whether genetics or environment shaped us, the answer is "both." If you had grown up two thousand miles away from your hometown, you would speak differently, have different interests, and possibly be on a different life path.

We know God placed us in our families as part of His plan. If He scripted the generations preceding each of us that carefully, wouldn't He also have considered the ancestors of His only begotten Son, Jesus? Not only that, but as He shaped the history of the people He would call His own—the Israelites—wouldn't He have considered how the place they lived and the culture they maintained would affect His greatest plan for humanity?

In this devotional, we will look deeply into the lives of people in the family history of Jesus, considering how their stories became His story and how all their promises came true in Him. Maybe it will help you love, appreciate, forgive, cherish, and be a little more gracious to your own family. Certainly, it will point you to God's perfect plan in Jesus, which made all the difference for us.

GETTING STARTED

This devotional contains thirty days of content, broken down into sections. Each day is divided into three elements—discover, delight, and display—to help you grow in your faith.

discover |

This section helps you examine the passage in light of who God is and determine what it says about your identity in relationship to Him. Included here is the daily Scripture reading and key verses, along with illustrations and commentary to guide you as you learn more about God's Word.

delight |

In this section, you'll be challenged by questions and activities that help you see how God is alive and active in every detail of His Word and your life.

display |

Here's where you take action. Display calls you to apply what you've learned through each day's study.

> **Each day also includes a prayer activity at the conclusion of the devotion.**

Throughout the devotional, you'll also find extra articles and activities to help you connect with the topic personally, such as Scripture memory verses, additional resources, and quotes from leading Christian voices.

SECTION 1

PATRIARCHS

God chose Abraham and his family to become His chosen people. He gave them a name, a home, and the identity that they were His. They weren't the mightiest, but God made His name and His power known through them. Most notably, this family would be the ancestors of His most amazing gift: Jesus.

MORE THAN JUST A LIST

discover |

READ MATTHEW 1:1-17.

An account of the genealogy of Jesus Christ, the Son of David, the Son of Abraham . . .
—Matthew 1:1

Matthew started his story of the life of Jesus Christ with a list of Jesus's ancestors. To us, that might seem strange; few of us know the names of our relatives more than a couple generations back. But to the Israelites, that list of family heritage was everything. Their ancestry told of their faith, their traditions, and their God.

You might recognize some of the names on this list. Some have an honorable reputation; some were called "evil." Your family probably has some good and bad in it too. There are names who are famous, like Abraham and David. There are also some names on there that you've probably never heard and are pretty sure you're pronouncing wrong. That might be like your family too!

What we see in this list is that none of it was an accident or random or left to chance. What this list of people indicates is that God has had a plan all along to introduce His Son into the world. God used all the people on this list to bring His plan together. Here is where it hits home for you: you are not an accident, or random, or left to chance either. God has a plan for you too. That plan also includes the family you come from.

There are probably things about your family you don't like. I'm sure Jesus felt the same way. But God can use everything about you—even the parts of your life that you aren't proud of—to bring together a glorious plan for His glory and kingdom. No situation or person is beyond the reach or ability of God to redeem, and the list of people we read today proves it.

delight |

Circle three names in today's passage that you instantly recognize. What do you know about their lives?

Underline three names in today's passage that you don't know well. How can you dig more deeply into their lives?

display |

Write down the names of people from your family of origin that you know well. Then write the names of family members you've met or somewhat know, but not well. Take a few minutes in silence and ask the Lord to give you a heart of compassion and faithfulness to your family—good, bad, and ugly. Take time to pray for your family: for salvation, for God's favor, for His mighty power in their lives. Consider how you might help or encourage someone on your list. Call or text one of them and tell them you love them.

Lord, just as You created Jesus's family according to Your amazing plan, You also have an amazing plan for my family. Help me to be the kind of family member that loves, helps, serves, and speaks the truth in love. Guide us in Your will and forgive us where we stray off the path. Amen.

DAY 2

WHEN BELIEVING SEEMS CRAZY

discover |

READ GENESIS 15:1-6.

Abram believed the Lord, and he credited it to him as righteousness.
—Genesis 15:6

God had first appeared to Abram (later called Abraham) in Genesis 12, promising that He would make him into a great nation, blessing not only Abram and his people but all people on earth (see vv. 1-3). As a seventy five-year-old man, those promises may have seemed unbelievable, but Abram believed. He uprooted his family, traveled hundreds of miles, and settled down in the place God had led them.

Fast forward ten years: Abram had done what God had called him to do, but he still didn't have any children. And in order for one to be a great nation, one must have at least one offspring. In today's focal passage, when God appeared to Abram again with another promise, Abram's response sounds like unbelief: "You haven't done the first thing you promised yet." Abram was looking around at his current situation, expecting something different. He thought at that time he'd be a father, so was God trustworthy?

God didn't try to back out of His promise or back away from it: again, He promised that Abram's heir would be his son. On top of that, God raised the promise: Abram would have so many offspring no one would be able to count them. The eighty five-year-old Abram could have rolled his eyes and walked away, thinking that God wouldn't follow through and make good on His promise, but he didn't. He believed God, and God credited that belief to him as righteousness.

delight |

What do Abram's question and statement in reveal about his faith (see vv. 2-3)?

What command did God give Abram in this passage? What promises did He give Abram?

How did God use nature to point to His promise?

display |

The unending surf of the ocean reminds us of God's never-ending love. The vastness of space reveals His unending power and authority. The itsy-bitsy measurements of our cells and the components within them reveal God's attention to detail. Just as God used the stars to reveal His promise to Abram, God can use anything in nature to remind us of His character. Take some time today to interact with God in nature: take a walk, take photos of flowers, try to race a dog, or sit under the stars. Praise God for who He is and how you can see Him in this world He gave us.

Father, You made amazing promises to Abram and he believed You. You've made amazing promises to me, too: You'll be with me, You'll love me, You'll guide me, and You'll give me peace. As I find your promises in Scripture, please give me the faith to believe You too.

When Laughing Isn't Funny

discover |

READ GENESIS 18:1-15.

But the Lord asked Abraham, "Why did Sarah laugh, saying, 'Can I really have a baby when I'm old?' Is anything impossible for the Lord? At the appointed time I will come back to you, and in about a year she will have a son."
—Genesis 18:13–14

We're not really sure why the three travelers caught Abraham's eye on this day. Perhaps he didn't get much foot traffic near his house; maybe he was hospitable, a common trait in the Ancient Near East at this time. Or maybe he could see something different about these three strangers and wanted to show them respect.

Abraham didn't just set out the 2000 BC equivalent of chips and salsa; he had Sarah make homemade bread, he butchered and cooked a goat, and he offered some cheese. What a spread. Then the Lord, speaking through the men, set a deadline to the promise He'd made long ago: within a year, Abraham and Sarah would have a son.

Instead of leaping with joy, though, Sarah laughed scornfully. She looked at her own body, and Abraham's, and considered the words of the Lord to be foolish. But nothing—nothing!—is impossible for God. His plan often doesn't match our plan, and His ways are not our ways (see Isa. 55:8-9), but we can trust His Word and His power, even in situations that seem like they are impossible.

delight |

How did Abraham show respect and honor to his guests? Why do you think he treated them this way?

How did God respond to Sarah's laughter? Why?

display |

God brings people into our lives: the new kid at school, the checkout lady at the grocery store, the teacher you love, or the uncle you've never really talked to. In every situation, we're called to be kind, respectful, and engaging. Not only might we develop lifelong relationships, but we may also hear a truth from God from them. As you go about your day, consider how you can offer your time, your attention, and your hospitality to strangers, friends, family, and beyond. As you spend time in conversation, laughter, and fun, praise the Lord for the blessings others bring.

Lord, You arrange our days, You give us joy, and Your promises are true. Just as You gave Isaac, whose name means "laughter," to Abraham and Sarah, You prove Your faithfulness as Your Word comes alive in our lives. Help us to put our faith and our joy in You, trusting Your love and Your timing for us.

THE WORST TEST EVER

discover |

READ GENESIS 22:1-18.

"And all the nations of the earth will be blessed by your
offspring because you have obeyed my command."
—*Genesis 22:18*

Abraham had waited . . . and waited . . . and waited for the son God
had promised. Isaac was his name, born when Abraham was one
hundred. The child of the promise became the child of Abraham's heart.
We can only imagine the gut-wrenching pain in Abraham's stomach
when God told him to offer Isaac as a sacrifice.

We might think the Bible would then say, "Abraham knew at this point
that God was completely crazy and vowed never to listen to Him again."
But that's not what Abraham did. He got up the next morning, loaded
up the supplies for a sacrifice, and set out for the place God instructed
him to go.

Abraham and Isaac made their way up the mountain. The tension is
clear even in Scripture: Isaac looked around and realized they had
everything for a sacrifice except, well, the sacrifice. But Abraham's faith
in God never wavered. Isaac was the son God had promised, and he
believed that if the sacrifice were required, God could raise Isaac from
the dead (see Heb. 11:19).

God spared Isaac and provided a ram in his place. But through the test,
Abraham learned something of utmost value: God can be trusted, and
Abraham was brave enough to obey.

delight |

What did Abraham's actions reveal to God (v. 12)? What did Abraham learn about God in this passage (v. 14)?

Look carefully back at verse 11: who stopped Abraham from slaughtering his son? What do you observe about God in this instant?

display

God asked for a mighty display of faith from Abraham. But we must remember that when the time came for His own Son to be sacrificed, God did not substitute a ram. No, God was willing to let Jesus die so that we might have eternal life. God will never ask you to love, give, help, serve, or sacrifice more than He already has. Commit today to following His instructions with faith and courage. As you reflect on these words, ask God what He would have you do today and go do that immediately.

Father, I see Abraham being faithful when You called him to do what seemed to be impossible. Help me, like Abraham, to hear Your voice clearly and obey immediately. I'm sure Abraham was fearful and nervous and full of doubt, but he chose to believe You and Your Word. I choose to do the same; give me the faith to believe You with my whole mind, body, heart, and strength.

GOD'S ESCALATOR

READ GENESIS 28:1-22.

Then Jacob made a vow: "If God will be with me and watch over me during this journey I'm making . . . then the LORD will be my God."
—Genesis 28:20-21

Abraham's son Isaac had two sons: Jacob and Esau. These twins were as different as night and day, and they fought like cats and dogs. When Jacob tricked Esau (and Isaac!) to steal the family blessing, he realized his best plan was to run away before Esau killed him. (Not kidding.) Jacob had often been deceitful and selfish, yet God had promised that His chosen people would come through the lineage of Jacob. Surely this liar wouldn't receive the promise, right?

Jacob had fooled a lot of people, but he couldn't fool God. On his journey far, far away from home, Jacob found himself all alone, sleeping on the ground. He dreamed of a stairway with angels traveling on it between earth and heaven. He then heard God speak, promising land, offspring, and the continued blessing He had given to Abraham. On top of all that, He also guaranteed that He would be with Jacob.

Shocked and afraid, Jacob realized the significance of the dream and God's promise—it was real, and God would follow through. Jacob turned the spot into an altar, clearly understanding the nearness of God and intentionally choosing to remember God's visit on his journey.

delight |

How did Isaac's blessing (vv. 3-4) reveal his faith and the faith he desired for Jacob?

In what ways does God's promise to Jacob (vv. 13-15) remind you of His promise to Abraham in Genesis 12:1-3?

Lion of Judah

display

Jacob didn't go looking for God; God came to Jacob in a mighty way. Though his actions showed him to be sinful and selfish, God had not given up on the man He had chosen to be the next generation of His promise to the descendants of Abraham and to the world. Are you like Jacob, going through life unaware of God's presence (v. 16)? Take time today to hear His voice, dwell in His presence, and obey His message to you. You may even want to journal or find a way to remember God's presence as you find Him there.

God, regardless of my past, You still have a plan for me. You are watching me, You are with me, and You are still faithful to keep Your promise to me. Help me to take my eyes off myself and turn them to You in faith and hope. Please give me spiritual eyes to see Your presence and faith to believe Your truth.

DAY 6
Epic Wrestling Match

discover |

READ GENESIS 32:24-32.

*"Your name will no longer be Jacob," he said. "It will be Israel because
you have struggled with God and with men and have prevailed."*
—*Genesis 32:28*

It had been a few decades since Jacob left home. God had most
certainly been with him, providing him with a large family and a
large flock. He was a successful, wealthy man, but his relationship
with God was still not solid: he still reverted back to his old, deceitful,
selfish ways.

Jacob gathered all he had and started back toward home. Though he
surely looked forward to seeing his parents, Isaac and Rebekah, there
was still one problem: Esau, the brother whose blessing he had stolen.
He didn't know what would happen when they came face to face. Did
Esau still want to kill him? Was God still with Jacob to protect him?

As darkness fell and Jacob pondered what would happen next, he
found himself wrestling with a man: it was God in a human body. And
though Jacob was tenacious and refused to let go, God was infinitely
more powerful and ended the wrestling contest with a touch to the
hip. Still, Jacob refused to let go until God blessed him. With a new
name and a new hope, God changed Jacob's identity and his outlook.
In response, Jacob acknowledged the presence, power, and lasting
impact of God.

delight |

What did Jacob's wrestling match with God symbolize?

What was the significance of changing Jacob's name after the wrestling match? How did Jacob's response reveal his awe and wonder?

display |

Jacob wrestled with God, but he didn't walk away from God. God is not afraid of our questions, doubts, or concerns, but He desires that we bring them to Him. The psalms are full of the honest questions and doubts of men of great faith who wrestled with God. As you spend time pondering God's Word today, bring Him your questions. Write them below or in a journal and pray them aloud. Cling to God in your questioning, believing that He will respond, He will hold on to you, and His presence will change you.

Lord, sometimes I'm afraid of tomorrow, just like Jacob was.
Sometimes I seek comfort and confidence in my friends, my family, or even myself. But I know You are the answer to every question I have. Give me the faith to cling to You in strength as we work through my struggles together.

MEMORY VERSE
RUTH 1:16

DON'T PLEAD WITH ME
TO ABANDON YOU
OR TO RETURN AND
NOT FOLLOW YOU.
FOR WHEREVER YOU GO,
I WILL GO,
AND WHEREVER YOU LIVE,
I WILL LIVE;
YOUR PEOPLE WILL BE
MY PEOPLE,
AND YOUR GOD WILL BE
MY GOD.

STRANGER THAN FICTION

discover |

READ GENESIS 38:11-26.

Then Judah said to his daughter-in-law Tamar, "Remain a widow in your father's house until my son Shelah grows up." For he thought, "He might die too, like his brothers."
—Genesis 38:11

There's an old saying that reality is stranger than fiction. The story of Judah and Tamar certainly speaks to the truth of that saying. Judah, the son of Jacob, had three sons. The first one married a woman named Tamar. That son was evil, and God took his life. The second son then married Tamar because that was his expected responsibility to his brother's widow. He was also wicked, and God took his life too.

Judah incorrectly assumed that the woman Tamar was the problem. He didn't realize the sinfulness that was running rampant in his family. He shielded his last son, Shelah, from marrying Tamar, denying God's command for the brother to take this wife. In a cringeworthy scene, Tamar dressed up, veiled like a prostitute. Judah slept with her, and she got pregnant with her father-in-law's baby. (Yes, this story is in the Bible!) When word got out that unwed Tamar was scandalously pregnant, she revealed who the father was: Judah. Judah saw his own sin clearly and took Tamar as his wife.

Jesus's family history wasn't perfect. This story of His ancestors shows that God is faithful to His promises even when we live far, far from Him. God always draws His people back to Himself through His grace and mercy.

delight |

How did deception and maintaining a respectable image lead to sinful heartbreak?

What does the word "right" (sometimes translated "righteous") in verse 26 mean?

display |

Sometimes we want to have our cake and eat it too: we sin, lie, and deceive, all the while pretending that we're living according to God's commands. Hypocrisy isn't limited only to Judah and Tamar; it's an overwhelming sin for many Christians. How do we overcome it? First, we choose to live in the light, without secrets or hiding. We keep Christian friends who hold us accountable and we find mentors to help us walk righteously. Take inventory of your walk today: are you in the light? Which friends hold you to your faith? Who is your Christian mentor? Write the names below of people who help hold you accountable and thank God for them.

Lord, this family You started for Jesus was quite a mess in this story. Sometimes my family is a mess too. Help me recall this story and remember Your mercy and grace, knowing You are loving and forgiving to Your children. Help me to show the same mercy and grace to my own family, striving to live righteously and point others to You.

Unexpected Heroine

discover |

READ JOSHUA 2:1-21.

*"Now please swear to me by the LORD that you will also show kindness
to my father's family, because I showed kindness to you. Give me a
sure sign that you will spare the lives of my father, mother, brothers,
sisters, and all who belong to them, and save us from death."*
—Joshua 2:12–13

So much has happened in Abraham's family since the story of Judah
and Tamar: Joseph was sold into slavery in Egypt, the whole family
ended up there, they became enslaved by the Egyptians, God sent
Moses to free them, and they had wandered in the wilderness for a few
decades. (It had been a big five hundred years.)

Moses had died, and now Joshua was just outside the promised land,
ready to lead God's people to the place He promised to Abraham
long, long ago (see Gen. 12:1-3). Joshua sent two spies into the city of
Jericho to get an inside look. They found a place to hide in the home
of the prostitute Rahab. She hid them and sent the soldiers looking for
them on a wild goose chase. Rahab risked her own life to protect the
spies because she believed in their God (see Heb. 11:31).

As they left to rejoin the Israelites, Rahab asked them to repay her
kindness with protection for her family. This unassuming hero protected
her family and revealed her faith in an unorthodox way, but she is still
an important part of the ancestry of Jesus.

delight |

What character traits do you see in Rahab? How did she demonstrate faith in God?

Upon what was the oath of protection made (see v. 12)? Why do you think this was important?

display |

Rahab had a sinful past; you do too. But your faith in God can be fresh and faithful today, just as Rahab's faith was revealed in her interaction with the spies. Rahab revealed her faith through her actions and her words; we do too. As you interact with others, consider how your words and actions acknowledge the Lord. Are you speaking words of faith or trust? Are you sharing what God has done in your life? Are you loving, helping, and forgiving as He commanded? If you're struggling to speak and live by faith, confess it and ask the Lord to help you walk His path today. Below, write two ways you can walk with faith today.

Lord, I see the faith in Rahab and I want to have that same kind of boldness in my own faith. I see that she was able to speak and live out her faith because she trusted You. Lord, help me to see You clearly, putting my trust in Your power and Your plan for my life.

Unmatched Loyalty

discover |

READ RUTH 1:1-18.

But Ruth replied: "Don't plead with me to abandon you or to return and not follow you. For wherever you go, I will go, and wherever you live, I will live; your people will be my people, and your God will be my God."
—*Ruth 1:16*

Some people in the genealogy of Jesus reveal particular characteristics of God. Ruth is remembered for her God-honoring loyalty. Born outside the land and people of Israel, Ruth had married an Israelite man whose parents lived in Moab, her homeland. The Moabites were descendants of Abraham's nephew, Lot—neighbors to the Israelites but worshipers of a false god.

Her father-in-law, husband, and brother-in-law died, leaving three women alone, helpless, and soon-to-be destitute. Her mother-in-law Naomi encouraged her son's wives to go back home and start a new life. One daughter-in-law did just that—after all, it was the smart thing to do by human standards. But Ruth refused: she wanted to be part of Naomi's family, Naomi's people, and a follower of Naomi's God.

Ruth's faith revealed her loyalty to Naomi and to Naomi's people. She was willing to leave everyone in her family, her homeland, and her culture behind in order to align herself with the God of the Hebrews. Ruth's life reveals that God called and used people who weren't Israelites in the Old Testament for His will and purposes.

delight

How did Ruth show faithfulness to Naomi? How did she show faithfulness to God?

Why did Naomi insist that her daughters-in-law go back to their homes? Why did Ruth refuse?

display |

Our heavenly Father demonstrated His loyal love throughout Scriptures. We are called to reflect His loyalty to the people in our lives. Whether we like them or not, and whether they return loyalty or not, we can point others to Jesus when our commitment stands out in our world and life. Who in your circle needs love, compassion, or help? How can you offer an encouraging word, a gentle hug, or the truth of Scripture? Even if your help is rebuffed or your friendship seems shaky, you can stay committed to being a friend and showing the compassion and loyalty of Christ. Write the name of one friend below that you can show loyalty to and pray for.

Lord, I confess at times I'm not very loyal. I can be selfish, picky, and selective in who receives my love and affection. But that's not the example You set. You overflow with compassion, grace, and loyal love. Please help me see Your loyalty to me and overflow with a reflection of that loyalty in my own life.

DAY 10
REAL HERO

discover |

"May your house become like the house of Perez, the son Tamar bore to Judah, because of the offspring the LORD will give you by this young woman."
–Ruth 4:12

Ruth and Naomi returned to Israel, and Naomi was back with her people. Though her husband's property still belonged to their family, the inheritance would have gone to her sons, who had died. Naomi and Ruth desperately needed a kinsman redeemer: a family member who would take the property as well as the responsibility of the two widows.

Ruth had provided food for herself and Naomi by gleaning grain at the field of a respected, godly man named Boaz. Romantic sparks flew between Ruth and Boaz, and by God's perfect placement, this generous man just happened to be a close family member; only one man could step in front of him in line to be the kinsman redeemer. Upstanding Boaz didn't try to weasel his way into marrying Ruth, but offered the land and wife to the closer relative. He declined, and Boaz saved the day.

When the town celebrated the happy turn of events for Naomi, they blessed her with the hope that her house would be like that of Perez, the son Tamar had through Judah. This prophetic blessing was looking back to the promise of God, flowing through Judah and his son Perez, down through the years to Boaz and his son Obed, the grandfather of David.

Lion of Judah

delight |

How did Boaz demonstrate that he was upstanding and respected? How did the people of the town demonstrate their excitement and respect for the new family?

How did Boaz's faithfulness to fulfill his obligation bless the life of both Naomi and Ruth?

display |

Sometimes our human tendency is to be lazy: we don't do the things we know we should do. Boaz was the opposite of lazy; he went out of his way to be responsible, upstanding, and obedient. Because of Boaz's character, his life was changed, and the lineage of Jesus flowed through his son. We, too, have a responsibility to God that involves being respected, hardworking, dependable members of our community. Look at your life today: where do you tend to be lazy? What is God calling you to do in faith? How can you respond today?

Father, there are so many qualities in Boaz that reflect You: wisdom, transparency, righteousness, and more. You've called me to reflect Your characteristics as well. Please show me where I'm not living a righteous life and give me the faith to walk in obedience. Help me to be heroic, like Boaz, through my everyday bravery and faithfulness.

SECTION 2

RULERS

God's chosen lineage for Jesus's family had gone through many generations and settings: from the wandering nomads of Abraham and his sons, to Joseph's descendants plunged into slavery in Egypt, and even through the conquest of the promised land and the time of the judges. Now God's people were demanding a king. While the people wanted an earthly king, God's plan was to bring about an eternal King: the King of kings and the Savior of the world.

Holy X-Ray Vision

discover |

READ 1 SAMUEL 16:1-13.

But the LORD said to Samuel, "Do not look at his appearance or his stature because I have rejected him. Humans do not see what the LORD sees, for humans see what is visible, but the LORD sees the heart."
—*1 Samuel 16:7*

When the Israelites began demanding a king, God gave them exactly what they wanted: a man taller and more distinguished than anyone else. He was a man named Saul. Saul's heart, though, was set on his own success and pleasing the people around him. God rejected Saul and directed his prophet Samuel to anoint a new king.

So as to not arouse Saul's anger, Samuel combined the kingly anointing with a town sacrifice, which would have been an expected assignment for a prophet. God led him to the town of Bethlehem and pointed him toward the household of a man named Jesse. Like Saul, Jesse's first son had the look of a king. But God revealed that He wasn't impressed with his external qualities. Instead of having a strong build and a chiseled chin, God was looking straight through to the heart.

Unfortunately, humans can't see the heart, and when Jesse was lining up his sons to meet the prophet, his youngest son, David, was out taking care of the sheep. But God, not Samuel or Jesse, was choosing this king. He knew exactly what He was doing. He was looking for a man after His own heart.

delight |

The Bible doesn't tell us specifically what made Eliab look kingly.
What do you think it was?

How did God confirm that Samuel had made the right choice in
anointing David as king?

display |

Because we live in a world filled with humans, we tend to focus on the external: looks, size, build, and more. We reflect this outward focus in the time and attention we give to our own appearance, whether it's exercising, a beauty routine, or simply complaining about how we look. But if God's looking at our hearts, the question becomes: How am I giving attention to what's going on on the inside? Am I filling my heart with things that promote love, peace, reverence for God, and a humble spirit? In the heart below, write three ways you can work on your heart so that it looks like God's. Today, intentionally spend as much time on your heart as you do on your outward appearance.

Lord, I know You see my heart, and it's not all good. I can be selfish, sinful, and I know that I fail You. But I know You have the ability to give me a new heart that seeks You above everything else. Today I turn my heart over to You; will you heal it, strengthen it, and hold it?

DAY 12

Big Enemy, Bigger God

discover |

READ 1 SAMUEL 17:1-52.

"Today, the LORD will hand you over to me. Today, I'll strike you down . . . Then all the world will know that Israel has a God, and this whole assembly will know that it is not by sword or by spear that the LORD saves, for the battle is the LORD's."
—*1 Samuel 17:46-47*

David had already been anointed king, but he still had a long way to go before he would wear the crown. As he waited, teenage David found himself tending sheep and serving as a messenger and food deliverer for his older brothers serving in King Saul's army.

When David showed up one day and heard the enemy's champion, Goliath, talking trash about Israel and Israel's God, he was offended. He began asking around to find out what would happen for the man who defeated Goliath, and that got him a personal invitation to see Saul. Unable to wear Saul's battle gear but full of confidence in God's ability to give him the victory, David headed to the battlefield.

David wasn't guilty of blind faith; God had already given him protection from the bear and the lion. God had given David the experience, the courage, and the tools to defeat a much-feared enemy. Though he was trained as a shepherd, he had already experienced the victory that only God would provide.

delight |

How did David offer encouragement to Saul? How did he offer his skills on behalf of God's people?

How did David's bravery inspire the rest of the troops (see v. 52)?

display |

David didn't need to go to Bible college or have missionary training to change everything for this dangerous situation for the Israelites; he needed only to share his testimony and take the step of faith. We can have the confidence and bravery of David when we do the same: tell others about what God has done for us and be willing to stand up for our faith and the faith of other believers. When you lead a Bible study, pray before a class, speak out on behalf of a mistreated kid, or encourage your teachers, you look and act like a David in your own world. In the space below, write out your testimony or story of faith. Be prepared to share it when the opportunity arises.

Father, sometimes I'm not brave. But I see now that bravery doesn't come from within but from You. Help me to look at Your power, Your faithfulness, and Your truths in order to find the courage to fight for my faith. Enable me to speak and act on behalf of who You are so that I can encourage others to fight also.

Sinful Spiral

discover |

READ 2 SAMUEL 11-12.

David responded to Nathan, "I have sinned against the Lord." Then Nathan
replied to David, "And the Lord has taken away your sin; you will not die."
—2 Samuel 12:13

David had done so many things well since being anointed king. He'd triumphed over Goliath and managed to become king without being killed by Saul. He had the respect of his enemies and his neighbors, worshiped with all his heart, and seemed primed to go down in the annals of history as one of the greatest leaders of all time, led by and giving honor to God.

But one bad decision led to another worse decision, and unchecked bad decisions lead down a path you could never have dreamed you'd walk. David should have been at war with his men, but he was at home. He should have heard his servants say that Bathsheba was married to one of his mighty men, but he ignored it. He should have repented immediately after each sin, but instead, he chose to continue the cover-up until he was so far down his sinful path that he'd practically broken every one of the Ten Commandments: lusting, coveting, adultery, lying, murder, and more.

One thing we can say for David is this: when finally confronted with his sin, he didn't try to hide anymore. He confessed. His confession—agreeing with God—was the first step toward restoration. Being a person after God's own heart doesn't mean you're perfect. It means you have a tender heart that responds to the conviction of the Holy Spirit like David did.

delight

In your Bible, underline each of the sins David committed. What was his first mistake that led to this awful situation?

For each item you underlined, write below what he should have done instead of what he did.

Lion of Judah

display |

Our lives can quickly spiral into sinfulness just like David's did. When we start out somewhere we shouldn't be and ignore the people around us who are trying to speak wisdom and discernment over us, we're headed toward deeper and more painful sin. Instead, we must be proactive in our walk of faith. Ask yourself today: What areas of my life am I keeping a secret from everyone else? To whom do I go for godly advice and wisdom? How well do I hear God's correction and discipline? If you're unsure of the stability of your faith, today is the day to seek out a mentor. Write the name of someone you can seek out to mentor you below.

Lord, I see the pain that David caused himself for all his sin, but I also see the pain he caused Bathsheba. Help me to remember that the consequences of my sin never fall on me alone but reach out and hurt others too. Help me see my way out of temptation, Lord, and consider Your path for me as the only way.

DAY 14
One Wish

discover |

READ 1 KINGS 3:5-15.

"So give your servant a receptive heart to judge your people and to discern between good and evil" . . . Now it pleased the Lord that Solomon had requested this.
—1 Kings 3:9-10

Surely you watched a movie or read a book about a magic genie in a lamp and wondered what you might wish for: Riches? Intelligence? Freakish athletic skills? More wishes (if the loophole really exists)?

The closest experience anyone ever really had to being granted a wish was King Solomon, David's son and the next in the lineage of Jesus. After Solomon had offered an immense sacrifice to the Lord, God appeared to him and said the crazy magic words: "Ask. What should I give you?" (v. 5).

This wasn't a genie; it was God Almighty, Lord of heavens and earth. Literally everything is under His command. If there's anyone who could actually invite us to ask for anything, it's God. Solomon surely considered the same options we would want to ask, but then he did the wise thing: he considered God's plan for his life. Solomon was king and was obviously feeling overwhelmed with the responsibility.

So he asked for the thing that would honor God and help Solomon walk in obedience and glorify the Lord: a receptive heart to judge and discern. Only the Lord could give him that, but only a person focused on the Lord would have even asked it.

delight |

How did God honor Solomon with His offer? How did Solomon honor God with worship?

How did God respond to Solomon's request (see v. 10)? What did God do because of Solomon's request?

display |

Solomon could have considered his own wishes and desires when he made his request of God, but riches and power would have given him no power to rule. In acknowledging God's authority for his life, he chose instead to ask for the tools to walk obediently and honor God. Are you asking for those tools? Have you asked the Lord to help you love others, show mercy, be compassionate, or help without the desire to be repaid? Are you allowing God's Word and Spirit to be the authority in your life? Are you choosing the things of God over the things that honor you? In the space below, write a letter answering the question God asked Solomon in verse 5. What will you ask for?

Lord, I know I could use some wisdom. Like Solomon, You've given me a path and responsibility in my life. To do that well, I need Your ability to discern between right and wrong in my relationships, my chores, my desires, and my thoughts. Help me to honor You with my life as I choose to obey and love You with my heart, soul, body, and mind.

WHO ARE YOU LISTENING TO?

discover

READ 1 KINGS 12:1-24.

Then the king answered the people harshly. He rejected the advice the elders had given him and spoke to them according to the young men's advice.
—1 Kings 12:13–14

King David had handed the throne of Israel over to his son Solomon. Though he'd been given wisdom in abundance along with riches and peace, he made a huge mistake: he had married foreign wives who worshiped false idols. Idolatry crept into Israel, and God's chosen people began to reflect the practices of these pagan nations.

To be quite honest, the nation of Israel never recovered. Solomon's son who became king was Rehoboam, whose decision-making skills revealed that his father's wisdom had not made it to the next generation. As Rehoboam took over the throne of Israel, a group of citizens (led by a man named Jeroboam; no relation) came to the new king and asked him to lighten up on the taxes and the demands made by the government. Though that sounds like a reasonable request to us, Rehoboam declared he needed three days to decide if he'd do it or not.

The wise older men told Rehoboam to listen to the people; Rehoboam's young friends told him to ignore them and flex his muscle. Rehoboam made the worse choice, and ten of the tribes of Israel decided they wanted nothing to do with him. The nation was now split in two, with only the tribes of Judah (the family that would take us to Jesus) and Benjamin following the lead of Solomon's son.

delight |

Look closely at verse 8. What would you tell Rehoboam if you had been his friend?

How did the Israelites respond to Rehoboam's declaration (see vv. 16-19)?

display |

Rehoboam was the son of Solomon, the wisest man who ever lived. Yet the phrase, "Like father, like son" doesn't work in this situation. Though wisdom was spoken plainly to him, Rehoboam chose the path of selfishness and pride, and it cost him the kingdom. We, too, will face the same crossroads: will you follow the wise voice of the Lord or will you choose to satisfy yourself? God has given us His Word, His Spirit, and wise people at our fingertips. They are resources anyone can use if we simply accept His guidance.

In your Bible, search for three verses about wisdom and write them down below. How can you apply these truths about wisdom to your daily life?

Lord, there are going to be times when I don't know what to do. When that happens, I depend on You to put wisdom in front of me. Please give me the faith to see the right path and the courage to walk it. My wise choices might seem foolish to my friends, but I'm following Your path, not theirs.

Maybe the Worst?

discover |

READ 2 CHRONICLES 21:1-20.

Jehoram was thirty-two years old when he became king; he reigned
eight years in Jerusalem. He died to no one's regret and was buried
in the city of David but not in the tombs of the kings.
—2 Chronicles 21:20

If you read today's key verse without reading the entire passage, you
might think that the people of Israel had become hard-hearted or just
calloused. If this is how you feel, you should really go back and read the
first nineteen verses of 2 Chronicles 20. In it, you'd see that Jehoram
was perhaps the worst king. Ever. Anywhere. For starters, he killed all
his brothers as soon as he took the throne. He "did what was evil in the
Lord's sight" (v. 6), and he led his people to give themselves to idolatry
and to turn their backs on God.

Elijah the prophet sent him a letter, basically telling him that God knew
all he had done and would not permit his idolatrous evil any longer.
God incited the Philistines to go to war against Jehoram's people,
carrying off all his possessions and family. On top of that, he suffered
from a horrifying intestinal disease. Seriously . . . go read it.

The Bible describes many kings who ruled Israel and Judah after
Solomon; Jehoram just might be the worst of them all. Unsurprisingly,
no one mourned when he died, and they didn't even bury him with the
kings. It's such a pitiful story and a terrible life.

delight |

If Jehoram was so terrible (and he was), why do you think God let him rule for eight years? (See v. 7.)

How did Jehoram's sin affect the people under his rule? How did it affect the strength of his nation?

display

There are many godly examples of how to live by faith—Jehoram is not one of them. In fact, you could look at everything in his life and do the opposite. Though today's passage highlights the worst, consider this: every big sin starts as a little sin that is never confessed and repented. At some point, Jehoram knew he was living out of God's will but chose to stay there. That is never God's plan. He calls us to be aware of His commands, confess our sins, and turn from them. When was the last time you did that? Take a moment now and pause to make sure you have confessed your sins to God. Don't let them build up and lead to greater deeds of unfaithfulness like Jehoram.

Lord, I see clearly how one person's evil deeds can have horrible ramifications. Jehoram is the complete opposite of who You've called me to be and who I want to be. So that I don't stay on any path that would take me away from You, help me listen carefully to Your correction, repent of my sin, and choose to walk righteously again.

BUT THE LORD SAID TO SAMUEL, "DO NOT LOOK AT HIS APPEARANCE OR HIS STATURE BECAUSE I HAVE REJECTED HIM.

Humans do not see what the Lord sees, for humans see what is visible, but the Lord sees the heart."

STANDING BOLDLY

discover |

READ 2 KINGS 18:1-8.

Hezekiah relied on the LORD God of Israel; not one of the kings of Judah was like him, either before him or after him. He remained faithful to the LORD and did not turn from following him but kept the commands the LORD had commanded Moses.
—2 Kings 18:5-6

As a contrast to the evil of Jehoram, today we look at Hezekiah. Like David, he lived in a way that God declared righteous. He also went out of his way to remove the idolatry that had become part of the culture of Judah, taking down the places where they sacrificed to false gods and destroying anything that was taking glory away from God.

The people had even begun worshiping something that started out as a source of healing and redemption. In Numbers 21, God's people had chosen to live in sin and had received punishment from God in the form of snakes. God, willing to forgive, told Moses to make a snake and mount it on a pole; anyone who looked at it would recover from the snake bite. Over time, the people had turned Moses's snake into an idol, given it a name, and were worshiping it.

Hezekiah saw this false idol and broke it into pieces. For his faithfulness, he was rewarded with the presence and power of the Lord. No one before or after was like Hezekiah: bold in his faith and unafraid to confront the sin of his world.

delight |

What actions proved Hezekiah's devotion to obeying the Lord?

How was Hezekiah remembered? How does that contrast with the lasting memory of Jehoram?

display |

You may see a little of yourself in both Jehoram (maybe the worst) and Hezekiah (one of the best). You find yourself walking in victory and faith one day, defeat and sin the next. Our lives reflect the nation of Judah: we waver. However, we have a merciful, loving God who is always ready to lead us, forgive us, help us, and love us. His mercies are new every morning, and we start each day with a fresh dose of faith when we connect with Him in His Word, prayer, and worship. Commit each morning to hearing God and choosing to obey Him. In the space below, write out a plan on how you will continue to connect with God through His Word, prayer, and worship.

Father, Hezekiah looks a little bit like me on my best days. Help me to see the pattern of his life—standing up for You and standing against idolatry—and choose to incorporate it into my everyday activities. You were faithful to Hezekiah; You've been faithful to me. Help me to follow You faithfully in response.

DAY 18
Grace and Forgiveness

discover |

READ 2 CHRONICLES 33:1-20.

When he was in distress, he sought the favor of the LORD his God and earnestly humbled himself before the God of his ancestors. He prayed to him, and the LORD was receptive to his prayer. He granted his request and brought him back to Jerusalem, to his kingdom. So Manasseh came to know that the LORD is God.
—2 Chronicles 33:12-13

A few days ago you read about Jehoram, who might have been one of the most evil kings of Judah. Today's king, Manasseh, is his competition for the title. Like Jehoram, Manasseh promoted idolatry in Jerusalem. But Manasseh went even further to thumb his nose at God, setting up false idol worship even in the temple of the Lord (see 2 Kings 21).

But the end of Manasseh's life contrasts with that of Jehoram. God allowed the Assyrians to attack and capture Manasseh because he repeatedly refused to listen to the word of the Lord. Distressed because he was captured with hooks and bound, Manasseh "sought the favor of the Lord his God and earnestly humbled himself before the God of his ancestors" (v. 12).

Manasseh had been an utterly horrible king and had led God's people to do unbelievably terrible things. Yet God, who is full of mercy, listened to his prayer and brought him back to his throne in Jerusalem. Manasseh then revealed his repentance in undoing all the foreign gods and idolatry he'd promoted. He led his people to serve the Lord. God's mercy does amazing things in the lives of those who genuinely repent.

delight |

Why do you think it took this worst-case scenario to finally bring Manasseh to his knees?

How do we know that Manasseh's heart was truly changed?

display |

Manasseh could likely look through the list of God's commands and check them all off: "Yep, I broke that one. That one too. That one more than once." His brazen idolatry was devastating not only to his own life but also to the people he ruled. But genuine repentance is powerful; regardless of sin, a changed heart and confession re-opens the pathway to God and His rule. If you're hiding from God because of your sin, stop. Go to Him in prayer, confess your sin, and turn away from the life you led. He will listen.

In the space below, write out a definition of "repent." If you need to look it up in a dictionary, that's fine. Then, take some time and examine your heart. According to your own definition, have you truly repented of your sins?

Lord, Your grace is truly amazing. Only You would see a man commit so many terrible sins and still forgive him. Father, I'm sinful too. I'm probably not as visibly idolatrous or murderous as Manasseh, but my sin is still there. I confess my sin; please strengthen me to turn away from things that do not honor You.

THE BEST OPPOSITE

discover |

READ 2 KINGS 23:1-25.

Before him there was no king like him who turned to the LORD with all his heart and with all his soul and with all his strength according to all the law of Moses, and no one like him arose after him.
—2 Kings 23:25

When you were a little kid, your teachers taught you opposites: dark, light; happy, sad; tall, short. In the Bible version of opposites, we add a new pair of words: Jehoram, Josiah. Josiah was eight years old when he became king, but by age eighteen he realized that they had been ignoring the Lord's law; in fact, they didn't even know what it said.

Josiah set out to right the wrongs that had been committed for generations. First of all, he had the scrolls with God's law read to all the people, oldest to youngest. Next, Josiah re-dedicated himself to the Lord's covenant and to obeying His commands. He then set out to destroy every trace of idolatry from the kingdom, destroying, burning, and tearing down anything that would take his people's eyes off the Lord.

He set the people back to observing the Passover and kicking out people who practiced witchcraft. Josiah had heard the word of the Lord and listened to it with his mind, heart, actions, and soul. After Jehoram and Manasseh, it may have looked like the lineage to God's Son would turn sour; however, there is always hope for the next generation to obey the Lord.

delight |

What words would you use to describe Josiah based on his actions and reaction to God's Word?

What characteristics of Jesus do you see in Josiah?

display

Few people have such a bold reaction to God's Word. When Josiah heard all the commands of the Lord and realized they had been living disobediently for generations, he could have thrown up his hands and said, "What can I do? I'm only eighteen!" But he didn't. Instead, he set out to use his authority and influence to change his world. We're called to do the same thing; we have God's Word, and our confidence to obey it can spread like wildfire. Read it, study it, memorize it, meditate on it, and live it. No matter how young you are, you can change your world too. Start by memorizing the verses found in this book. See pages 26-27, 60-61, and 88-89 for help.

Lord, Josiah was born into a wicked family, but that didn't keep him from following You. Help me to grow up in Your Word, into Your Spirit, and into the life You've called me to live. I seek Your guidance and leadership, and I know I can find those things in the Bible. Thank You for Your Word and for people who stand with me in walking by faith.

Who Are You Looking At?

discover |

READ HAGGAI 1:1-15.

*Then Zerubbabel . . . and the entire remnant of the people obeyed the
Lord their God and the words of the prophet Haggai, because the
Lord their God had sent him. So the people feared the Lord.*
—Haggai 1:12

Between Josiah's story and today's passage, much had happened with God's people: even though Josiah had done everything he could to lead them back to the Lord, they continually chose to disobey and turn to idols. So God gave them over to their enemies, and the nation was sent into exile. After a time, they were allowed to return to what had been their homeland, but it no longer belonged to them; it was ruled by a foreign kingdom called Medes and their King Darius.

Still, they reinhabited Jerusalem, going about normal life. They built farms and homes for themselves, but no one really thought about rebuilding the temple. Even when God attempted to get their attention by making their plants fail and their clothes seem inadequate, they never turned their attention to God or asked Him what was going on.

God then sent word through the prophet Haggai: rebuild My house. Jesus's ancestor Zerubbabel and the rest of the returned exiles obeyed the words of the prophet. God had inspired them to obey, and they did exactly what he said. As the temple was restored, they found their relationship with God restored as well. The people feared the Lord and God was with them.

delight |

What excuses had the people given for not rebuilding the Lord's temple?

In what way did God's people put their own desires and needs in front of the desires of God?

display |

Even when life isn't going as we had hoped, God is King. Even when our situation is not ideal, He is still on His throne. Even when we are struggling just to get our lives in order, we don't have the option of ignoring the King of our lives. The descendants of Jacob had turned their attention inwardly and had ignored their responsibility to God. We tend to do the same when we get busy or stressed—we don't turn our eyes to the Lord. Take time today and solemnly ask, "Lord, what have You called me to do for You? How can I honor You today?"

Father, You are King not only of my life but also of this universe; how could I ever neglect what You have called me to do? I know You want me in Your Word, You want me to show love, and You want me to glorify You with my life. So I ask You today: put me in a situation where I can do just that. Help me to live for You.

SECTION 3

Parents

Friends are important. So are teachers, coaches, extended family members, and people at church. But no one has more influence on our lives than our parents. And regardless of how you feel about your parents or how you respond to them, your interaction with them will affect your entire life. Consider the weight of parental influence as you learn about Jesus's parents over the coming days.

DAY 21
YES, LORD

discover |

READ LUKE 1:26-38.

"See, I am the Lord's servant," said Mary. "May it happen to me as you have said."
—Luke 1:38

We don't know many details about Mary's life, but we know much about her faith. Mary was most likely a teenage girl, engaged but not married, when the angel Gabriel appeared to her. Though his warning seemed encouraging and warm ("Greetings, favored woman! The Lord is with you," v. 28), she was deeply troubled: Why had an angel come to visit her? Could this really be good news? Just as you would have been curious and a little suspicious, so was Mary.

Then the angel revealed his message: Mary would be the mother of the promised Messiah! The One the people had been waiting for would be her Son! The Israelites had been praying for this Messiah for centuries, waiting for the fulfillment of the promise God had made to Abraham, down to David, and all his descendants. The angel's words in verse 33 assured her that this Son would be the One they had expected and hoped for.

How would all of this come to be? Did it make sense to Mary? No, not really. But Mary heard the angel's words in verse 37—"For nothing will be impossible with God"—and believed them. She submitted to God's will, which was unclear to her, with all of her unsure heart, confident that the God who was with her ancestors would be with her too.

delight |

How did the angel's greeting foreshadow his message? Why do you think Mary was "deeply troubled" (v. 29)?

What else might you have expected Mary to ask the angel? What would you have asked?

display

We remember that God—all-knowing, all-powerful, eternal—sees things that we can't. In our day 11 study, we read that God could see David's heart. We don't know exactly what He saw in Mary, but we know He saw something that made her His person for this unbelievable task (see v. 28). When she responded to the angel's wild message of God's crazy plan, we see her heart too. Mary one hundred percent believed God and submitted to His path for her life. That same God has a plan for your life too. Do you trust Him for it? Have you submitted to His instructions?

In the space below or in another place, draw a map of your life so far. Along the route, from your birth up to today, map out the major events and things that have happened. Consider God's involvement in these events and reflect on the path He has brought you on.

Lord, I see Mary's willing spirit and I really must confess: I am often afraid to be that brave in my faith. You call people around the world away from their own plans for their lives. But I also know that You have an amazing plan for me. Even when I don't understand all the details, please give me the faith to say yes to whatever it is You have for me. Yes, Lord!

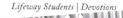

Faithfully Obedient

discover |

READ MATTHEW 1:18-25.

But after he had considered these things, an angel of the Lord appeared to him in a dream, saying, "Joseph, son of David, don't be afraid to take Mary as your wife, because what has been conceived in her is from the Holy Spirit. She will give birth to a son, and you are to name him Jesus, because he will save his people from their sins."
—Matthew 1:20-21

As amazed as we are by Mary's faith, Joseph's story is inspiring as well. When news got out that Mary was pregnant and Joseph knew he wasn't the father, he thought there were two explanations: she was lying or she had lost her mind. Either way, Joseph was an honorable man and decided he was going to end their engagement quietly. In that day, the men in the relationship had all the power and could end relationships very publicly. Joseph was going to do it quietly so that more disgrace didn't come Mary's way.

God wanted to make His plan perfectly clear to Joseph, so He sent an angel to explain it to him. The angel revealed God's plan and how it fulfilled the Scripture from the prophet Isaiah.

Joseph could have woken up, chalked the dream up to some spicy food, and continued on with his life. But he didn't. Like Mary, he believed God. He married her and named the baby Jesus, just like he was instructed. This whole story reveals Joseph's character. It also shows how carefully God chose the people who would raise His Son here on earth.

delight |

Where do you see words from Joseph in these passages? Where do you see acts of faith?

In both Mary and Joseph, God chose people who said yes to Him, even though what He was asking was hard. Where are you saying yes to God in your life?

display |

Joseph was faithful to obey God. As crazy as God's plan seemed to Mary, consider how ridiculous it seemed to Joseph. Following God could mean risking everything: his reputation, his relationships with his family, and more. But when God spoke, Joseph listened. He honored the Lord and His plan by doing everything He told Joseph to do. How immediate and complete is your response to God's instructions? Do you listen carefully and obey instantly? God has given us all the path for life in His Word: love, help, serve, do, show. How well are you walking down that path today? In the space below, write out one way you are either loving, helping, serving, doing, or showing your obedience to God's direction for your life.

Lord, Joseph is a great role model for me. I see his strength and his courage as he obediently listened. And it's not like You called him to an easy task, Lord; no, that path was going to be very tough. May I, like Joseph, trust You fully and obey You immediately.

Honor in Waiting

discover

READ LUKE 1:34 AND MATTHEW 1:24-25.

He married her but did not have sexual relations with her until she gave birth to a son.
—Matthew 1:24-25

Many people today consider God's commands and instructions to be old-fashioned or overly restrictive. They struggle with God's directives to submit, be kind, help, forgive, and love. Perhaps the most disregarded teaching of the Bible is God's design for sexual relationships.

The Bible is clear: sexual immorality, or sex outside of marriage, is a sin (see 1 Cor. 6:18, 1 Thess. 4:3-5, Gal. 5:19). Mary and Joseph understood God's standard and had not allowed sexual temptation to ruin the purity of their relationship. This even gave Mary some confusion when Gabriel told her she would be the mother of the Messiah: how would that be possible when she was a virgin? (See Luke 1:34.) Joseph honored God and Mary by respecting her and obeying God's design. They did not begin their sexual relationship until after Mary delivered Jesus.

Some may argue: What's the big deal? Would anyone really know? Did it really matter? YES. God knows the heart and the mind of each person, and He also knows what we do with our bodies. As an overflow of our trust in the Lord, we obey His commands, even if we think it doesn't matter or is old-fashioned. Today's passage reminds us that God is honored when we glorify Him with our bodies.

delight |

How did Joseph and Mary's obedience to God guide and direct their relationship with each other?

Go back and re-read Matthew 1:20-23. How did Joseph's actions reveal his faith?

display |

One of Satan's most prolific lies is this: no one else obeys God this way. He leads us to feel isolated, weird, and ridiculous when we choose to obey God's design. The desire to have sex outside of marriage has always been prevalent in society; we simply see it more clearly in today's technological world. But God's standards have not changed with the times. What steps are you taking to guard your heart and mind against temptation, particularly in your dating relationships? Write those down today and read them regularly.

Lord, You are Lord of creation and Lord of my life. As my Creator and King, You have the right to tell me how to walk obediently. I choose to listen to You—not our culture, not popular opinion, and not other people. I accept Your standards for my dating relationships. I understand that my faith is revealed in my life, and I commit to walking faithfully in Your commands today.

DAY 24
Blessed Is She

discover |

READ LUKE 1:39-45.

In those days Mary set out and hurried to a town in the hill country of Judah where she entered Zechariah's house and greeted Elizabeth.
—Luke 1:39–40

We would probably be right in thinking that Mary was overwhelmed with the news that Gabriel brought to her: she would have a baby, and it would be God's Son. She had found favor with God, but there's a good chance others didn't believe her. Can you imagine: "God's Son? Mary, you're just lying to us!" Even Joseph didn't believe her until the angel set him straight.

But God, who is so good to us, gave Mary a relative who would believe her and encourage her: Elizabeth. Like Mary, nobody expected Elizabeth to be pregnant; it was a miracle. Also like Mary, an angel had delivered the news about who the baby would be and how he was part of God's plan. But unlike Mary, Elizabeth was too old, not too young.

Regardless of their age difference, Mary hurried to Elizabeth's house. Upon her arrival, Elizabeth's baby jumped when Mary's voice was heard. This was a perfect foreshadowing of John the Baptist (Elizabeth's baby) being the forerunner to Jesus. Elizabeth's words of encouragement and truth gave Mary strength and courage to face the next scary steps in her faith journey.

delight |

What gives you the indication that Mary was excited to see Elizabeth?

Who are people in your life, like Elizabeth, who encourage you? How can you let them know that you are grateful for the encouragement they have been to you?

display |

Elizabeth said these beautiful words to Mary: "Blessed is she who has believed that the Lord would fulfill what he has spoken to her" (v. 45). Prophetic and beautiful, Elizabeth allowed the Holy Spirit to guide her words of encouragement and truth. Yes, Mary would face hard times in walking the path God had for her. But at that moment, she needed to hear exactly what Elizabeth told her: "You are blessed! You believed God! He is faithful!" We, too, can make a habit of speaking encouragement and hope to our friends and family. Ask the Lord to guide your words today and find someone to encourage.

Father, I see this beautiful friendship between Mary and Elizabeth, and I know it's Your plan for friends to look like this. Give me friends and mentors who will encourage and pass along the hope of Your Word. Also, help me to be an encouraging, truth-speaking friend to the people You put in my life. Help me to build others up.

And Mary said: "My soul magnifies the Lord, and my spirit rejoices in God my Savior"

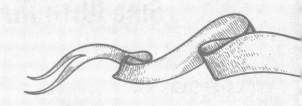

MEMORY VERSE
—LUKE 1:46-47

Sing With Mary

discover |

READ LUKE 1:46-56.

And Mary said: "My soul magnifies the Lord, and my spirit rejoices in God my Savior."
—Luke 1:46–47

According to Luke, these words of Mary come immediately after Elizabeth's words of encouragement and hope (see Luke 1:45). Mary had just received the news that she would have an honor no other woman in all of creation would have: she would give birth to God's Son, the Messiah.

Yet Mary didn't do any of the things we might expect: she didn't get prideful, didn't gloat, didn't let it go to her head. In her song, she praised God, proclaiming He is the "Mighty One" whose "name is holy" (v. 49), speaking of His "mercy" (v. 50), His mighty deeds (see v. 51), and His power over those who consider themselves to be powerful.

In contrast, Mary pointed to her own humility: she realized that any acknowledgment she received was because of what God did. She pointed to the fact that God satisfies the hungry and remembers Abraham and his descendants. Yes, Mary was looking back at the fact that God made the promise to Abraham almost two thousand years earlier, realizing it would come true in the baby she would deliver!

Mary's song is an outpouring of her soul (see v. 46), the invisible part of her emotions that connected her with the Lord. God's tangible working in her life led her to spontaneously praise and exalt the Lord.

delight |

How many times does Mary mention God's mercy? What does that reveal to us?

What does it take to be humble? What about Mary's song reveals that she was humble?

display |

Mary referred back to the words of Isaiah in her song (see Isa. 2:12) when she mentioned that God is against the lofty or prideful. We have no room for pride; God alone is our Creator, Sustainer, Helper, Protector, Guide, and more. When Mary looked at the blessing of God in her life, she realized that it was all God's power and mercy. Nothing she did could have led to such an outcome. We, too, should humble ourselves as we see God plainly. He is the source of everything. He deserves our glory and praise. Today, write or speak praise to God for His power, mercy, or grace in your own life.

Lord, I don't know that I am always humble like Mary. But I'm starting to see clearly that You are God and You are worthy of my worship. I see in Mary's song that the better I see You and know You, the more humble I will be. Help me to see You clearly, worship You in truth, and walk in holy reverence of who You are.

DAY 26
Obedient Parents

discover |

READ LUKE 2:21-24.

And when the days of their purification according to the law of Moses were
finished, they brought him up to Jerusalem to present him to the Lord.
—Luke 2:22

Mary and Joseph were both Jews, meaning they were descendants of Abraham and followers of the Law that God gave to them through Moses. In Exodus 13, God instructed His people to consecrate (or set apart) every firstborn to Him by presenting an animal sacrifice. This would be a reminder to the parents that God deserves the first and best of each part of our lives.

Mary and Joseph were obedient to the Lord, giving Jesus the name the angel told Joseph, following God's law for purification, and bringing Him to Jerusalem to be dedicated. We see that Joseph and Mary were honorable to the Lord, obeying His commands and living in accordance with His standards of righteousness.

God's best plan is for families to have godly parents, and He blesses parents who live in such a way that honors Him. But we saw in the lineage of Jesus that even children who don't have godly parents can still live according to God's plan. Anyone can seek God for salvation and follow Him in faith.

Lion of Judah

delight |

What does it mean to dedicate something to the Lord? Look back at the situation surrounding Exodus 13, where this law first appears. What is the significance of it? (See vv. 14-15.)

How did Mary and Joseph's actions reveal their obedience?

display |

Growing up, many kids say things like, "When I'm an adult, I'm going to eat ice cream at every meal!" You may have similar ideas about when you are an adult as well. But no believer ever outgrows being obedient to God. Followers of Jesus are called to obey Him by faith regardless of their age. Even if you eat ice cream for dinner, you should never disregard God's instructions. In what area are you living disobediently? Take some time to confess that to the Lord today. Like Mary and Joseph, your obedience must be lived out in your life.

Lord, I know that You call me to obey, and disobedience isn't acceptable. Please help me see the things I do that displease You. Let me practice walking in obedience now instead of waiting until I am an adult. I want to honor You with my mouth, my attitude, my heart, and my thoughts.

Listen and Obey

discover |

READ MATTHEW 2:13-23.

After they were gone, an angel of the Lord appeared to Joseph in a dream, saying, "Get up! Take the child and his mother, flee to Egypt, and stay there until I tell you"... So he got up, took the child and his mother during the night, and escaped to Egypt.
—Matthew 2:13-14

Maybe as a child you heard the expression, "God gave you two ears and one mouth; you should listen twice as much as you talk." That's not in the Bible, but it summarizes Joseph perfectly. The books of Matthew and Luke both give us insight into his life, but there is not one recorded word that Joseph spoke in the Bible. However, we see over and over again that he heard God clearly and obeyed.

God protected Mary and baby Jesus through Joseph's careful listening. In today's passage, the wise men had just left, and Herod realized he'd been tricked. To make sure the prophecy would never be fulfilled and no child would take his throne, Herod ordered every boy under age two to be killed. Yet just before that decree, the Lord had sent an angel to Joseph, instructing him to take his family and flee to Egypt. Without a moment to spare, Joseph got up, gathered his family, and did just that. Over and over, we find stories of Joseph receiving instruction and him obeying. When God spoke, Joseph listened. What a powerful testimony for a faithful man of God.

What do you learn about Herod from this passage? What do you learn about his son Archelaus?

In what ways were some Old Testament passages fulfilled in today's Bible reading?

display |

We might protest, "Well, Joseph had an angel delivering God's messages to him; of course he listened." But we who hold the Word of the Lord in our hands also have the ability to know what God is saying every day. God has spoken clearly, and He speaks to us even today through His Spirit and His Word. The question, then, is whether or not we actually listen and obey. Consider your heart: What is God saying to you right now? What will you do about it today? The more carefully we listen and obey, the more often we'll hear His voice. Write below one thing God is telling you to listen to and obey.

Lord, I know what You're saying to me: love, help, serve, forgive, reach. Your instructions are quite clear. And yet I don't always do those things. I'm often selfish in that I just want to do what I want to do. I confess today that I don't always obey You. Please give me ears to hear and faith to obey You each day.

Worship and Worry

discover |

READ LUKE 2:21-24.

Every year his parents traveled to Jerusalem for the Passover Festival.
—Luke 2:41

For all of the wonderful characteristics of Mary and Joseph, we must remember that they were human: flawed, imperfect, struggling people who tried their best but didn't always get it right. Basically, they were just like us. We should start today's passage with the last verse: "They did not understand what he said to them" (Luke 2:50). Though they were adults and he was a twelve-year old, they really didn't fully grasp the significance of His life and His purpose at that point.

They also lost Jesus. They had been to Jerusalem and were headed back home, assuming he was in the large group of travelers they were with. But when they got a day away and realized Jesus wasn't with them, we can only imagine the panic: "I thought He was with you!" They hurried back to Jerusalem, finding Him not scared and alone, but hanging out with the experts, discussing the Word of God.

We should cut Mary and Joseph some slack. They weren't perfect parents, but they were doing their best to raise a perfect child. What we need to not miss are those opening words: "Every year they traveled to Jerusalem for the Passover" (Luke 2:41). These imperfect parents wanted their child to know God and worship Him. We have seen how their faith guided their lives, and they desired for their entire family to come to know the God that they so faithfully loved and followed.

delight |

According to verse 47, what did the teachers and experts of the Law think about Jesus?

How did Mary and Joseph respond to finding Jesus? What do their words reveal about Jesus?

display |

God saw the hearts of Mary and Joseph and chose them to be the earthly parents of His Son, yet He knew they weren't perfect and wouldn't understand everything. The same is true of your parents: they have been chosen by God to raise you, but they won't get it right every time either. As Christians, we choose to know and worship God, and we also choose to show grace to our parents when they don't fully understand or make the right decisions. Consider telling your parents or guardians how awesome they are today, and maybe throw in a hug. No matter what life at home is like—wherever that may be—you can pray for the people who take care of you. Jot down a few ways you'll pray for them today.

Holy God, I pray for my parents or guardians today. I know they aren't perfect, and neither am I. I pray that you would give them wisdom and help me to have the humility to obey them. May I honor You as I honor them.

Lion of Judah

How to Grow Up

And Jesus increased in wisdom and stature, and in favor with God and with people.
—Luke 2:52

We know that Jesus was twelve years old when he was accidentally left behind in Jerusalem. Today's passage follows immediately after that story, so we know that Jesus's teenage years were marked with Him growing in four distinct ways.

First, He grew in wisdom. We know that the fear of the Lord is the source of wisdom (see Prov. 1:7). We gain wisdom as we make decisions based on God's Word. Secondly, He grew in stature, meaning he physically grew taller, stronger, and more mature. Third, He grew in favor with God, meaning He walked obediently with His heavenly Father, obeying His commands and choosing to observe all the things God had instructed His people to do. Finally, He grew in favor with people. This means that young people and adults alike enjoyed being around teenage Jesus. They saw His life was full of good things.

Jesus didn't grow in these four ways all on His own. Verse 51 tells us clearly that He was obedient to His parents. Even Jesus—fully God, the embodiment of all things holy—needed to obey His parents. In learning to listen to them and walk according to their teachings, He revealed to believers the importance of submitting to human authorities.

delight |

What do you observe about Mary in this passage? What do you think she was keeping in her heart?

What do you think Jesus did to increase His wisdom?

display |

The teenage years were when Jesus grew from a boy to a man—not just physically but also spiritually and relationally. These years are the time for you to grow up in all these ways as well. Increasing in stature may happen without much effort on your part, but increasing in wisdom, favor with God, and favor with people takes intentional decisions. How you structure your days—with Bible study, worship, and prayer—and how you interact with others—in your words, attitude, and actions—will determine whether or not you increase in the ways that matter most. Are you growing up? Why or why not? Write out your thoughts and answer below.

Lord, I know that the teenage years won't last forever, and it's not okay to look and act like a teenager for the rest of my life. Help me to do the things that will help me to grow up into an adult, physically, spiritually, relationally, and emotionally. Help me use the wise believers in my life to guide me to take steps of maturity in all these areas.

DAY 30
Final Hours

discover |

READ JOHN 19:25-27.

When Jesus saw his mother and the disciple he loved standing there, he said to his mother, "Woman, here is your son." Then he said to the disciple, "Here is your mother."
—John 19:26–27

For our last devotion in the lineage of Jesus, we fast forward to the end of His earthly life. Yesterday's passage described Him at age twelve, and today's Scripture looks at the last day of His life. In Luke 2, He was obeying His parents, and in John 19, He is providing a home and a protector for His mother as He took His last breath.

We're not sure what happened to Joseph or when he died, but after Luke 2:51, we don't hear anything else about him. Bible historians think he likely died sometime in Jesus's teenage or early-adult years. Whatever happened, Mary was surrounded by her girl friends at the foot of Jesus's cross. Not only was her Son being killed, but she likely would have become destitute without Him.

Jesus made sure that didn't happen. Looking at the only disciple brave enough to come to His cross, Jesus assigned John ("the disciple he loved," v. 26) the role of accepting Mary as his own mother, providing for her and watching over her. We know now that Mary would be in good hands because John served Jesus for many years to come. We can also imagine Mary and John comforting each other with stories and memories of Jesus long after He had risen from the grave and ascended back to heaven.

delight |

Who was with Mary at Jesus's cross? What do you know about these other women who were there? (Look them up in a Bible dictionary if you need some help.)

Why do you think John called himself "the disciple [Jesus] loved?"

display |

If anyone had the right to focus on Himself for a few hours, it would have been Jesus, especially at this point His life. Not only had He been unjustly tried and crucified, but He was carrying every sin on His back as He died for us on the cross. Yet even in His final hours, Jesus's deep respect for His mother was evident. Our respect and honor for our own parents must be lived out as well. Do you honor your parents with your words, your attitude, and your actions? Are you kind, helpful, and encouraging? Do you look for ways to be a blessing to your parents? If not, it's time to start taking those steps.

Lord, there are times when I don't show my parents the respect they deserve. And I know that even when my parents are not at their best, they should still be honored. Help me to love them, respect them, and honor them because that's how You are glorified. You have promised to bless the generations that honor You; I want to choose that path.

ALL THE STARS ABOVE

At this point, you're probably pretty familiar with Jesus's family tree, at least as far back as Abraham. Still, tracing the lines through the various names can be tricky. After all, God did promise to make Abraham's descendants as numerous as the stars. To review the people in Jesus's lineage, let's chart some stars. In each star, you'll see a name you might already know. Draw lines to show marriages (if applicable) and children (see Matt. 1 for help). Then, using your Bible and this book, below each star, write out one character trait you think best describes that person.

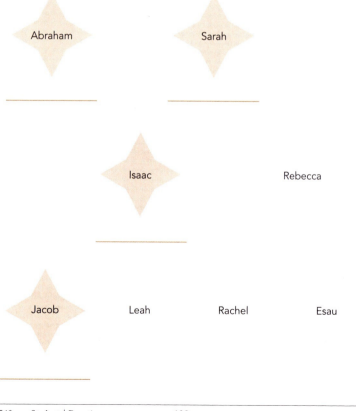

Tamar

Judah

_____

_____

Rahab

Salmon

_____

Boaz

Ruth

_____

_____

David

Bathsheba

_____

Solomon

_____

Rehoboam

_____

Jehoram (Joram)

_____

Hezekiah

_____

Manasseh

_____

Josiah

_____

Zerubbabel

_____

Joseph

_____

Mary

_____

Elizabeth

_____

Jesus

_____

Think about the people who have raised you up in the faith—your faith family. These might be family members, mentors, church leaders, or even friends. Starting with the person who told you about Jesus, create your own family tree, going back two or three generations. End with your name. Complete the same exercise, drawing stars around the names in your line and noting one characteristic you believe each of these people have. Ask questions of your faith family if you need to!

Once you've finished both family trees, highlight the characteristics that stand out most to you—ones you want to show up in your own life. Using your list as a guide, pray, "God make me a person of . . . (fill in your characteristics here)." Someone who came before you was faithful to tell you about Jesus. Pass the message on and see God's faithfulness in the new branches on your own faith family tree.

NOTES